Runaway Train

For Miles Butcher

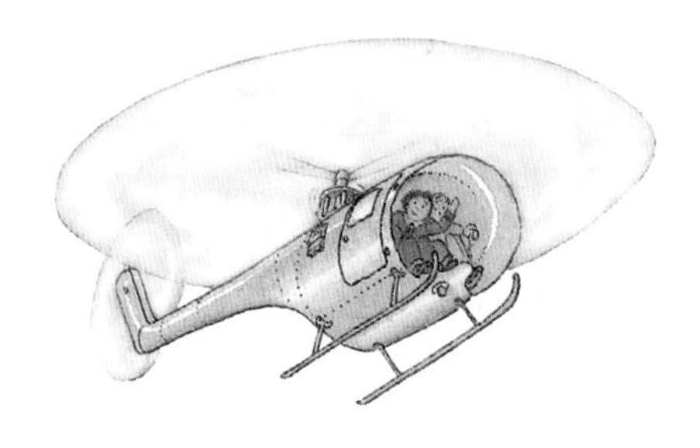

RUNAWAY TRAIN
A RED FOX BOOK 978 0 099 38571 4

First published in Great Britain by Julia MacRae,
an imprint of Random House Children's Publishers UK
A Random House Group Company

Julia MacRae edition published as *The Runaway Train* 1995
Red Fox edition published 1997 as *The Runaway Train*.
Red Fox edition re-issued 2009

27 29 30 28 26

Red Fox Books are published by Random House Children's Publishers UK,
61–63 Uxbridge Road, London W5 5SA

www.**randomhousechildrens**.co.uk

Addresses for companies within The Random House Group Limited can be found at:
www.randomhouse.co.uk/offices.htm

THE RANDOM HOUSE GROUP Limited Reg. No. 954009

A CIP catalogue record for this book is available from the British Library.

Printed in China

LITTLE RED TRAIN

RUNAWAY TRAIN

Benedict Blathwayt

RED FOX

Duffy Driver overslept.
Everyone was waiting at the
station for the little red train.

VISIT
HORLOCK

When Duffy was ready to start, he saw an old lady running down the platform. "I'll help you," he said. But he forgot to put the brake on and the little red train set off down the track . . .
Chuff-chuff, chuff-chuff, whoo . . . oooo

T15 J13

Duffy saw a lorry. "Stop!" Duffy shouted. "I must catch up with the runaway train!"
"Jump in," cried the lorry driver and off they went after the little red train . . . *Chuff-chuff, chuff-chuff, whoo . . . oooo . . .*

. . . until they came to a traffic jam.

Duffy saw a boat. “Ahoy there!” Duffy shouted. “I must catch up with the runaway train!”

“All aboard,” cried the boatman and off they all went after the little red train . . . *Chuff-chuff, chuff-chuff, whoo . . . oooo . . .*

. . . until the river turned away from the railway.

Duffy saw some bicycles. “Help!” Duffy shouted. “I must catch up with the runaway train!”

“Jump on,” cried the cyclists and off they all went after the little red train . . . *Chuff-chuff, chuff-chuff, whoo . . . oooo . . .*

. . . until they ran into a flock of sheep.

Duffy saw some ponies. "Whoa!" Duffy shouted. "I must catch up with the runaway train!"
"Up you come," cried the riders and off they all went after the little red train . . . *Chuff-chuff, chuff-chuff, whoo . . . oooo . . .*

. . . until the ponies could go no further.

Duffy saw a tractor. "Halloo!" Duffy shouted. "I must catch up with the runaway train!"

"Get on then," cried the farmer and off they went after the little red train . . . *Chuff-chuff, chuff-chuff, whoo . . . oooo . . .*

. . . until they were spotted by a helicopter pilot.

"My last chance!" gasped Duffy. "I must catch up with the runaway train!"
"Climb in quick," said the pilot and Duffy climbed in, while the lorry driver, the boatman, the cyclists, the riders and the farmer all stood and watched . . .

as Duffy caught up with the runaway train . . . *Chuff-chuff, chuffitty-chuff, whoo . . . oo . . . oo*

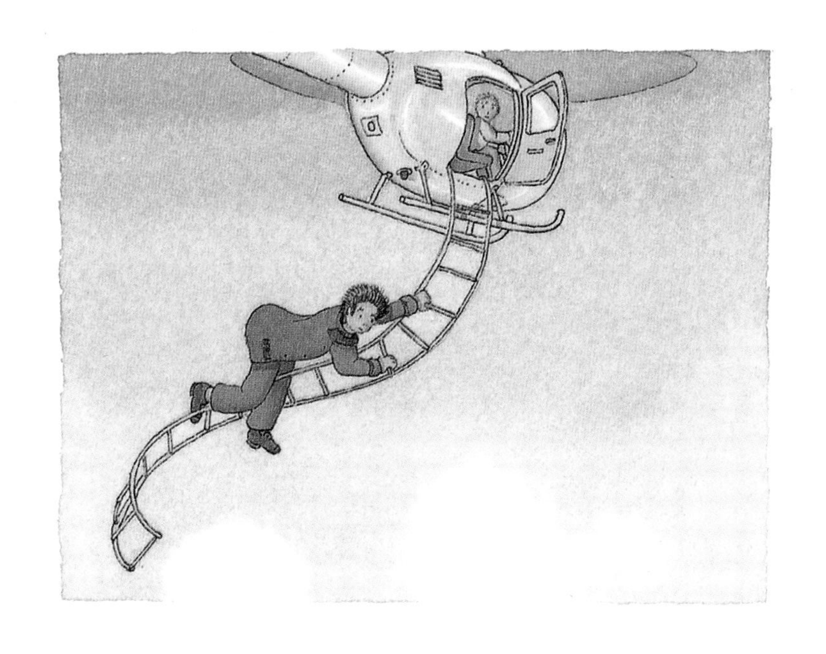

And Duffy Driver drove the little red train into the station at Sandy-on-Sea and spent a lovely lazy afternoon on the beach before he had to drive back home again.

FOR LUCK

Chuff-chuff, chuffitty -chuff, whoo . . . eee . . . eee . . .

More exciting stories to enjoy!

Picture Story Books

Faster, Faster, Little Red Train (also available as a Story Book and CD)
Green Light for the Little Red Train (also available as a Story Book and CD)
The Great Big Little Red Train (also available as a Story Book and CD)

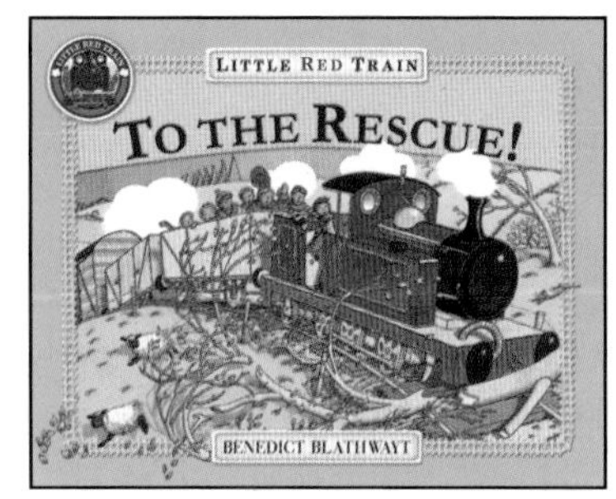

(also available as a Story Book and CD)

(also available as a Story Book and CD)

Board Books

One, Two, Three with the Little Red Train – An Adventure with Numbers
Little Red Train Goes Chuff, Chuff, Chuff – An Adventure with Noises

Gift Books

Stop That Train! – A Pop-Through-the-Slot Book
Little Red Train Adventure Playset
The Runaway Train Pop-up Book
The Runaway Train Sticker Frieze
The Little Red Train Gift Collection
The Runaway Train Book and DVD